PUFFIN BOOKS

Trouble with the Fiend

Sheila Lavelle was born in Gateshead, County Durham, in 1939. When she was a child she spent all her time reading anything she could get her hands on and from the age of ten began to write plays, stories and poetry.

She married in 1958 and had two sons. When her children started school she returned to the writing that had been put on hold and sold some stories to a magazine. At the same time she trained as a teacher and taught in infant schools in Birmingham for ten years. After an illness Sheila Lavelle gave up teaching to write full time. Her first book, *Ursula Bear*, was published in 1977.

Sheila Lavelle now lives in a cottage near the sea in Galloway, Scotland, with her husband and two Border collies. She is now also a grandmother! Her days are spent writing in the morning and walking her dogs in the afternoon.

Other books by Sheila Lavelle

MY BEST FIEND
CALAMITY WITH THE FIEND
THE FIEND NEXT DOOR

For younger readers

FETCH THE SLIPPER
HARRY'S AUNT
URSULA BEAR

Trouble with
the Fiend

Sheila Lavelle

PUFFIN BOOKS

PUFFIN BOOKS

Published by the Penguin Group
Penguin Books Ltd, 27 Wrights Lane, London W8 5TZ, England
Penguin Books USA Inc., 375 Hudson Street, New York, New York 10014, USA
Penguin Books Australia Ltd, Ringwood, Victoria, Australia
Penguin Books Canada Ltd, 10 Alcorn Avenue, Toronto, Ontario, Canada M4V 3B2
Penguin Books (NZ) Ltd, 182–190 Wairau Road, Auckland 10, New Zealand

Penguin Books Ltd, Registered Offices: Harmondsworth, Middlesex, England

First published by Hamish Hamilton 1984
Published in Puffin Books 1995
3 5 7 9 10 8 6 4

Copyright © Sheila Lavelle, 1984
All rights reserved

Made and printed in Great Britain by Clays Ltd, St Ives plc

Chapter One

THE day we poisoned Laurence Parker was one of the worst days of my life. I wish I had never let myself get mixed up in Angela's rotten scheme. I wish I had just stayed peacefully at home and played with my puppy, Daniel, and worked on my holiday project. Sometimes I wish I had never even met that Angela Mitchell next door because whatever we do together always seems to land me in trouble.

It was the holiday project that started it all, I suppose. What we had to do was collect six different wild flowers, press them, and stick them on a card with their names written on. I was pushing a few shrivelled old flowers around on the kitchen table, trying to remember what they'd looked like before I'd squashed them flat in my mum's copy of *The Complete Works of William Shakespeare*, when my dad came to see what I was doing.

"Is that a speedwell or is it a harebell?" I asked him hopefully. But he only gave my flowers a baffled look and scratched the little bald patch on the top of his head.

"Don't ask me, Charlie girl," he said. "They're all weeds to me. Your mother might know." My name is Charlotte really, but I'm called Charlie most of the time, thank goodness.

"Why don't you get Angela to help you," suggested my mum, coming to look over my shoulder. "It's one of the things she's good at, flowers and stuff. Like her dad."

My dad gave a loud snort.

"What? That little fiend?" he said. "Good at flowers? I bet she rips the petals off one by one, just for fun." My dad is always calling Angela a fiend. Ever since that time at school when I wrote "Angela Mitchell is my very best FIEND." It was only a spelling mistake, but my dad likes to pretend that it wasn't.

My mum started to wash up the lunch dishes while my dad finished the last of the chocolate mousse when she wasn't looking. I thought it was quite a good idea to ask Angela about the flowers because she does know a lot more than me, especially about the wild kinds. So I swept them all into a plastic sandwich box and went to wake Daniel up out of his basket.

Daniel wriggled and bounced so much at the prospect of a walk that I could hardly get the lead on him. At last I managed to get him ready and we set off together down the drive.

Angela only lives next door, but it still took us the best part of ten minutes to get there because Daniel had to sniff every single pebble and blade of grass on the way. He's still only a puppy, and I have to be a bit patient with him.

We eventually arrived at Angela's back door. I dragged Daniel away from Uncle Jim's vegetable marrows and tied him firmly to the handle of the dustbin. I knew I couldn't take him in the house because Auntie Sally won't have him inside any more. Not since that time he made a big puddle right in the middle of *The Sunday Telegraph* which was lying on the floor. But he was only a very little puppy at the time, and anyway how was he supposed to know that *The Sunday*

Telegraph hadn't been left on the floor especially for him to spend a penny on?

I patted Daniel on the head and told him I wouldn't be long, and he licked my hand to show he didn't mind waiting.

"Come in," called Auntie Sally's voice when I knocked on the back door. So in I went.

And there they all were, Auntie Sally and Uncle Jim and Angela, and they were all scoffing the most luscious-looking strawberries you ever saw.

"Hello, sunshine," said Uncle Jim cheerfully. "We're just finishing lunch. Come and have a few strawberries. They're fresh out of the garden this morning."

I didn't need asking twice. I still had some room left after my sausages and mash and chocolate mousse, so I pulled back a chair and sat down. But Angela was too quick for me.

"Charlie doesn't like strawberries," she announced. "They bring her all out in spots." And she picked up the bowl and tipped the last few strawberries into her own plate.

I watched her as she sprinkled on the sugar and covered them with cream. I opened my mouth to say something, but she gave me such a kick on the shin under the table that I didn't dare.

"Never mind, Charlie," said Auntie Sally. "You can help me clear up while Angela finishes them off." So I had to clear the table and dry the dishes and try to stop my mouth from watering while Angela scraped her plate noisily with her spoon.

"You greedy cat," I said, as soon as we were outside. "You know how much I love strawberries." Angela put on her most astonished expression.

"Oh, Charlie. I'm sorry," she said, her blue eyes all wide and innocent. "I must have been thinking of somebody else."

I didn't believe her. But there wasn't much I could do about it. I wanted to keep her in a good mood so she would help me with the flowers. Anyway, there was no time to argue about it because just then we heard the most almighty crash from behind us. A neighbour's cat had come strolling into the garden and Daniel had set off after it, forgetting he was tied to the handle of the dustbin.

So after we'd picked up the tin cans and the kipper bones and the potato peelings and wiped all the tea leaves off Daniel's face, we wandered out into the street. And I could have hugged my friend Angela, because even though she had finished her own flower project she agreed to help me with mine.

"We'll get rid of these, for a start," she said, taking one look at my collection and tipping the whole lot under the hedge. "I'll help you find some nice fresh ones, and I'll press them for you in my flower press."

Because of course. Angela, who always gets whatever she wants, has got one of those posh wooden presses with all the shiny nuts and bolts and sheets of clean white blotting paper.

"But you're not thinking of bringing that stupid dog of yours with you, I hope," she added, looking down at Daniel, who was busy trying to wind his lead round our ankles.

"He's not stupid," I said. "He's very intelligent. My dad said so."

"Well, he looks stupid." said Angela, tossing her hair impatiently. "And he's got a stupid name. Fancy anybody calling a spaniel Daniel.

It's the silliest blooming thing I ever heard of."

Daniel looked up at the sound of his name, and gazed at us lovingly. I fondled his silky ears, and his tail wagged like mad.

"I think it's a lovely name," I said. "It was my dad's idea."

Angela groaned. "I might have known," she said scornfully. "Anyway, he's not coming with us, and that's that. He'll only get in the way."

So I took Daniel back indoors. I plonked him in his basket, patted his head, and tried not to look at the reproachful look in his eyes.

Angela was waiting for me outside and we set off together towards the meadows by the river. And it didn't take me long to cheer up because it was such a sunny day with the sky all blue and the birds singing and the trees in their green summer dresses. We found loads of different kinds of wild flowers, and I was astonished that Angela knew so many of their names.

"My dad's been teaching me," she explained. "He seems to think it'll make me more interested in gardening. Some hope." She suddenly darted forward. "Look, Charlie. Here's some gallant soldiers."

They looked just like daisies to me, and I wished I knew more about them. The names were such lovely ones. Gallant soldier and rosebay willowherb and monkey flower and shepherd's purse and lords and ladies and forget-me-not and lots more. I filled my box up in no time, and it was when we were climbing over a stile beside a tall hawthorn hedge that we found the little purple and yellow flowers.

"Woody nightshade," said Angela. "Look, it's got berries on it as well."

She picked a few of the sinister red berries and that funny look started to come into her eyes. The look that means she's having one of her ideas.

"We could have some fun with these," she said.

"What are you up to?" I said suspiciously. "What sort of fun?"

Angela looked at the berries in her palm. "Well, I think it was woody nightshade that was used in the olden days. As a sort of drug. I think it sends people to sleep." She narrowed her eyes and gave me that wicked grin of hers. "We could try it on somebody, for a joke. Miss Menzies, for instance. Or that fat fool Laurence Parker." And she began to laugh and dance about.

Well, of course I argued like mad. I told her it was a horrible trick and much too dangerous, but she refused to listen to a single word. I nagged her all the time she was collecting the berries and I kept on at her all the way home until at last she got furious with me.

"Oh, shut up, Charlotte Ellis," she said. "Don't be so WET."

And I did shut up then because she'd called me Charlotte and she only does that when she's really mad with me. When we got home Angela ran next door to fetch her flower press, while I went inside and spread out all my lovely new flowers on the kitchen table.

It was nice to be home. I got a big welcome from Daniel and a kiss from my dad who was watching football on the telly. And the kitchen smelled all warm and spicy because my mum was baking a cherry cake for tea.

Well, I waited and waited and it was nearly a whole hour later when at last Angela turned up. She burst in the back door without knocking, looking dead excited and pleased with herself.

In her arms was a big cardboard box, and the flower press was sticking out of the top.

"Hello, Angela," said my mum, sliding the cherry cake out of its tin on to a plate. "You're just in time for a slice of cake. Just give it a few minutes to cool."

"Yummy," said Angela, rolling her eyes. "And please can Charlie and me have it in the garden? My mum's packed us a picnic tea and Laurence Parker is coming at five o'clock."

My mum stared hard at Angela and then at me. I got a sudden nasty sinking feeling in my stomach.

"You don't like Laurence Parker," said my mum. "You've hated him for years. Why should you want to invite him to tea?"

"It's time we tried to make friends, isn't it?" said Angela, grinning all over her face.

My mum was still staring at us suspiciously, but I shrugged and made my face go blank. We started sorting the flowers, and Angela helped me to put them in the press. But I could see that her mind wasn't on what she was doing. As soon as we had arranged the last bit of blossom between sheets of blotting paper she grabbed her box of picnic stuff and hurried me outside.

"I've been round to Laurence Parker's house," she hissed, hopping gleefully from one foot to the other. "I've told him we want to be friends and he's coming to tea. I've squeezed the berries and I've got the stuff here." And from the pocket of her skirt she pulled a tiny bottle of evil-looking dark red liquid.

I stared at the bottle and I didn't half feel awful.

"It will be OK, won't it?" I said faintly. "We don't want to hurt anybody, do we?"

"Oh, don't we?" said Angela wickedly, cackling like a witch, and that made me feel even worse.

Anyway, I knew there was no way I could stop her once she'd made up her mind, so I helped her to drag the old furry rug out of the playshed and spread it on the lawn. Then we knelt down to unpack the picnic box.

Auntie Sally certainly knows how to make a nice spread. There were warm sausage rolls and ham sandwiches and slices of tomato and cucumber and packets of crisps and jam tarts and cans of coke and a whole box of those lovely Cadbury's chocolate biscuits. There were proper picnic plates and knives and forks and even a white cloth to spread it all out on. While we were busy my mum came out with a big wedge of her newly-baked cherry cake.

"That looks delicious, Auntie Liz," said Angela, with her sweetest smile, and my mum looked pleased.

"You've got quite a feast there," she said. "Enjoy yourselves."

As soon as my mum went back into the house Angela started to cut the cake into three slices.

"I'll cut two small bits and one big bit," she said with a giggle. "That greedy pig is sure to take the biggest bit. And it will serve him right."

She took the little bottle from her pocket and quickly sprinkled a few drops of the sticky red liquid over the largest slice of cake.

"Perfect," she said. "He'll never notice a thing, because of the cherries."

She hid the bottle away just in time, because just then Laurence Parker came shambling in through the garden gate, his hands stuffed into his trousers pockets and his feet shuffling on the gravel path.

"Hello, ladies," he said, grinning sheepishly. And I could see that he didn't half think it was a soppy idea to have tea in the garden with two girls. Angela must have bribed him with the thought of all that food.

He certainly brightened up when he saw the picnic all spread out on the cloth in the sunshine.

"Cor, this looks a bit of all right," he said, gloating. And without wasting any more time he threw himself down on the rug and started tucking in.

Well, you should have seen the way he stuffed himself, cramming in huge mouthfuls and dropping crumbs everywhere and spilling dribbles of coke down his fat chin. It was disgusting. I felt sick in my stomach and I couldn't eat a thing. Especially when I saw the way Angela was enjoying herself, chatting away merrily as if they'd been the best of friends all their lives. I kept on staring at that cherry cake. And the piece with the red stain on it seemed to be staring straight back at me.

And at last the awful moment came.

"Have some cake," said Angela, picking up

the plate and offering it to Laurence Parker. "Charlie's mum made it. It's delicious."

And of course Laurence Parker, being Laurence Parker, chose the biggest slice, took a great mouthful and chewed it down.

"It's yummy," he mumbled with his mouth full, spraying crumbs all over the cloth. "Best cake I ever tasted. Tell your mum . . ."

I never learnt what it was he wanted me to tell my mum. His mouth fell open and his eyes started to bulge out of his head. He clutched his stomach and a horrible moaning noise came from the back of his throat. Angela and I clung together in fright as he staggered to his feet and grabbed himself round the neck with both hands.

"AAAAAAAAGH!" he howled, lurching and reeling round the garden and banging into everything in his way. "AAAAGH! HELP! I've been POISONED!" And then he suddenly crashed down flat on his back with a great thud right in the middle of my dad's rhubarb patch.

There was silence for a moment. I looked at Angela and Angela looked at me.

"Flippin' heck," she breathed. She got up quickly and ran over to where Laurence Parker lay among the broken rhubarb stalks. She flung herself down and put her ear to his chest. When she looked up at me her eyes were all wide and tragic.

"He's dead," she whispered hoarsely. "We've killed him. It must have been *deadly* nightshade we gave him."

I turned and fled back to the house and my heart was thumping away like anything and I don't think I've ever been so frightened in my life. There was no sign of my mum in the kitchen, so I rushed into the sitting room where my dad had fallen asleep in front of the telly. I grabbed his shoulders and shook him hard and screamed in his ear.

"Dad! Dad! You've got to come quick."

"Wasser matter?" he said grumpily, almost tumbling out of his chair. I got him by the wrists and started to pull.

"It's Laurence PARKER!" I shouted. "We've MURDERED him. In the RHUBARB patch."

My dad took one look at my terrified face and made for the door. He dashed out into the garden with me close on his heels and we raced over the lawn and round the runner bean poles to the rhubarb patch.

There was nobody there. Not a soul. No Laurence Parker. No Angela. Nobody.

"He . . . was here a minute ago," I faltered lamely, feeling dead stupid, I can tell you.

"Well, he certainly isn't here now," said my dad crossly. "And whatever it was he was up to, he's made a right old mess of my rhubarb."

He went stumping back to his telly. I stood there for a minute, just staring at the ground. Then I went round to Angela's house.

"Hello, Charlie," said Auntie Sally, letting me in. "Looking for Angela and Laurence, are you? They're in Angela's sitting room. And I'd love to know what it is they're laughing about up there."

I went upstairs and opened the door of Angela's own little sitting room that Uncle Jim built specially for her over the garage. And there were Angela and Laurence Parker. They were hooting and shrieking and falling about and saying "Did you see her face?" and "She really fell for it, didn't she?" and they were making so much noise that they didn't notice me standing there in the doorway all grimfaced.

So I coughed loudly to make them look up, but when they saw my expression it only made them laugh even more.

"What was that stuff in the bottle?" I said, in the sternest voice I could muster.

"Ribena," Angela managed to splutter. "It was only Ribena, that's all. Laurence knew all about it. And wasn't his acting great? He should be on the telly." And they both collapsed with the giggles all over again.

I left them there and walked slowly home, feeling a proper idiot. You have to admit it was a good trick, though, when you think about it. Only I sometimes sort of wish it wasn't always me that got the worst of it.

Chapter Two

I'M not the only person Angela plays tricks on. She does it all the time, to everybody. Friends at school, my dad, her dad, Miss Menzies up the street, strange ladies in cafés, even teachers. And even our new teacher, Miss March, which takes some nerve, I can tell you.

Miss March is the games mistress and our class teacher as well. We all call her Quick March behind her back because she's just like a sergeant in the army. She's sort of square-shaped with short black hair and solid legs like tree trunks. She wears great thick spectacles like the bottoms of jam jars and she has a bellowing voice that you can hear from the other end of the playing field. And you should just hear the way she yells at us.

"You have sixty seconds to get changed, starting from . . . NOW!" she shouts, standing in the corridor between the boys' and the girls' changing rooms. And woe betide anybody who isn't in their shorts and tee-shirt and plimsolls by the time she blows that horrible shrieky whistle she wears on a green ribbon round her neck.

I was walking to school one Monday morning and I hadn't called for Angela that day, partly because I was still sulking with her for blowing up my mum's airing cupboard and spoiling our best sheets, and partly because the postman had just given me a letter with a London postmark and I wanted to read it in peace.

The letter was from my Uncle Barrie who teaches at a London comprehensive school. And I got a very nice surprise when I opened it because there was a five pound note inside as well as a belated birthday card and one of his funny poems. I was having a good giggle at the poem when I heard Angela's voice behind me.

"Charlie," she called. "Wait for me."

I waited until she caught up with me. She was all out of breath from running and she looked so pleased to see me that I hadn't the heart to be cross with her any more. We linked arms and walked on together and I started to tell her Uncle Barrie's poem.

"There was a young lady called Vickers
   Who rode on a pony to Twickers
   She rode round the town
   And when she got down . . ."

I stopped because I could see she wasn't listening.

"I've got something to tell you, Charlie," she said. "Only you must promise not to give the game away." She kept breaking out into chuckles and giving little skips in the air as we went along. "Do you promise? Cross your heart and hope to die?"

"You're up to something," I said sternly, stopping on the pavement and staring at her mischievous face. "Come on, Angela. What is it this time?"

"Wait till you see what's in my satchel," she said, giggling more than ever. "That Miss March is going to get the fright of her life." She started to tug at my arm. "Stop dawdling, Charlie. We have to get to school before she does."

We arrived at the school gates at twenty-five to nine and there was still hardly anybody about. We hung our blazers in the girls' cloakroom and then took our satchels along the corridor to the classroom. I hung mine on the back of my chair, but Angela went straight over to Miss March's desk and lifted the lid.

"Angela," I said, in a shocked voice. "What are you doing?" Nobody is ever allowed to open the teacher's desk, and Angela knows that perfectly well.

She ignored me completely and took a small cardboard box with a few holes punched in the sides out of her satchel.

"Come and meet Freddy," she said, grinning.

I moved forward cautiously, praying it wasn't a spider. Or a bat. I've got a thing about spiders and bats.

Angela took the lid off the box and out hopped a little green frog.

"Oh," I said, smiling with relief. "Isn't he sweet? Where did you get him?"

"He was hopping round the lawn when I got up this morning," said Angela. "I thought I would bring him for the nature lesson. But then

I had a better idea. I'll leave him in Miss March's desk and he'll hop out when she opens the lid and I bet she screams the place down."

I doubted that very much. Miss March is the sort of person who isn't frightened of anything. If she wrestled with a sabre-toothed tiger she would probably win.

"It'll take more than a frog to scare her," I said. "Anyway, I think it's cruel. That poor little thing needs to be out in the fresh air. I think you're mean and I'm not going to have anything to do with it."

Angela stuck her tongue out at me and her face went all sulky as I stalked off back to the playground with my nose in the air.

"Stuffy old spoilsport," she called after me. So I was surprised to see that she had got over her sulks by the time the bell went, and gave me a wink and a friendly smile as we all trouped in and took our places.

Miss March breezed in and rapped on her desk for silence. And I winced as I thought of that poor little frog sitting there wondering if the sky was falling on his head.

"Good morning, class," boomed Miss March.

And we all got to our feet and stood to attention like soldiers.

"Good morning, Miss March," we chorused dutifully, and everybody sat down. Miss March stood in front of the class and treated us to one of her nastiest smiles.

"A nice little surprise for you this morning, Class Five," she said. "Desk inspection." Our desks are supposed to be kept tidy at all times but of course we forget and let them get in a bit of a muddle. Miss Bennet always used to give us ten minutes to tidy up before desk inspection, but not Miss March. She's too mean. Sometimes I think she only does these sudden checks so she can grab the odd Mars bar or tube of Smarties that we're not supposed to bring to school.

Anyway, a great groan went rippling round the room and one or two people quickly lifted their desk lids and tried a crafty tidy up. But this wasn't allowed.

"All desk lids CLOSED," bellowed Miss March, and we all sank timidly in our seats and wondered who she was going to pick on first.

And of course she picked Laurence Parker, whose dad is the managing director of a sweet factory, and whose pockets are always crammed full of toffees and chocolates and stuff.

"Laurence Parker, you can be first," said Miss March, striding through the desks towards where he and I sat together in the middle row. Laurence Parker went red and I heard him say a very rude swear word under his breath. Then I saw him quickly raise his desk lid an inch or two and slide his hand inside. And before I knew what was happening I found a big crackly cellophane packet being shoved into my lap.

I looked down and my heart nearly stopped beating. Lying on my navy blue school skirt was a whole half-pound bag of Parker's chocolate Caramels. There was no time to shove them back because Miss March was already looming over us like a thunderstorm. I couldn't slip them into my desk as mine was sure to be the next one to get inspected. So I did the only thing I could think of. I scooped them up under my cardigan and held them against my ribs with my elbow, praying that Miss March wouldn't notice the bulge.

Laurence Parker's breath came out in a long whistle of relief. He opened his desk lid wide, looking smug as anything because the inside was as tidy as could be.

"Very good, Laurence," said Miss March. "I wish everyone could be as neat. Now let's have a look at yours, Charlotte Ellis."

I wasn't worried about my desk. I knew I'd given it a good clear-out last thing on Friday. So I got a nasty shock when I opened the lid and found, right in the middle, on top of my nicely arranged exercise books, a small cardboard box with air-holes punched in the sides.

"And what might this be?" enquired Miss March, pouncing on the box and waving it in the air.

"It's um . . . er . . . it's a box," I mumbled, turning pink and hunching my shoulders as I felt the bag of sweets start to slip out from under my elbow.

"I can see that," snapped Miss March, and the whole class tittered. "But what's in it?"

"Nothing," I whispered, looking daggers at Angela, who was laughing up her sleeve. "It's empty."

"Well, we'll soon see," said Miss March. And she opened the box and peered in. Everybody else craned their heads to look, but they were all disappointed because there was nothing but a few damp leaves and tufts of grass.

"I'm waiting for an explanation, Charlotte," said Miss March coldly. And I sat there not saying a word. I could hardly tell tales on my best friend, could I? Even if she had put the box in my desk to get me into trouble.

Miss March pressed her lips together in a grim line and handed me the box.

"Take that and put it on my desk," she said. "And you can stand in front of the class until you decide you have something to tell me."

I shuffled to my feet, feeling the slippery bag of sweets slide even further down inside my cardigan.

"And stand up straight," Miss March added impatiently. "You look like the hunchback of Notre Dame." And she got hold of me by the shoulders and gave me a good shake.

And of course that's when I finally lost my grip on the bag of sweets and it shot out of the bottom of my cardigan and clattered to the floor. Everybody laughed at my red face, and that spiteful Delilah Jones said "Oooh, Charlie Ellis," as if I'd stolen the crown jewels.

Miss March snatched up the sweets in triumph and took them back to her desk. She banged hard on the lid for silence.

"That's quite enough, everybody," she said. "As for you, Charlotte Ellis, you will stay in at playtime. And I shall want a full explanation of your behaviour. Your sweets are, of course, confiscated." And I held my breath as she opened the lid of her desk.

Well, that poor little frog must have been half out of its wits with all the banging because as soon as the lid was open it gave a great leap straight into Miss March's face. And Miss March let out such a shriek and jumped about half a mile in the air as if it was a nest of rattlesnakes in there and not just one little frog, and it just goes to show that even the toughest of people are usually frightened of something.

Anyway, it wasn't Miss March I was worried about. I was feeling sorry for the poor little frog. He had fallen to the floor and was now attempting pathetic little flopping jumps along the skirting board, cringing from the din everybody was making.

I didn't really stop to think. I ran out to the

front of the class and picked up the frog as gently
as I could. I popped him back into his cool leafy
box and put him safely away in my desk. But I
soon wished I hadn't.

The bedlam suddenly quieted and I looked
up. There was Miss March, charging towards me
like a rhinoceros, her face purple with rage. And
it kept going white and then red and then purple
again, like the disco lights at my Auntie Fiona's
wedding reception.

I won't tell you everything she said. But I can
tell you that it took a long, long time. I had to
stay in every playtime for a whole week, and
I had to write out one hundred times 'I must
not bring sweets to school,' and one hundred
times 'I must not play practical jokes on my
teacher'.

Laurence Parker was ever so grateful that I
hadn't told on him and he was as nice as pie to
me afterwards. He walked home with me from
school and he went with me to set the little frog
free in a cool, boggy patch of ground near the
Abbotsbrook stream. And he shared a whole box
of sugared almonds with me that he had hidden
in his blazer pocket in the cloakroom.

And who should come following us along the road, smiling away as if nothing had happened, but Angela.

"Get lost, Angela Mitchell," I said, in my best stuck-up voice. "I'm fed up with you and all the trouble you get me into."

And this time I really meant it. For a little while, anyway.

Chapter Three

I don't think Angela always gets me into trouble on purpose. Sometimes her ideas only go wrong by mistake. Like the time we burnt down her dad's garage so that he could get the insurance money. It wasn't her fault the garage wasn't insured. And it wasn't really her fault when we blew up the airing cupboard, either. At least I don't think it was.

It happened last winter, before I got my puppy, during that spell of freezing cold weather in January. I was in my bedroom, raiding my building society money box with the breadknife and getting nothing out of it except a few pennies and two pences, probably because that's all I ever put into it. And even when I include the two pound coins. I had left over from Christmas, and still only had two pounds eighty-nine pence. Which wasn't much for a birthday present. Especially for my dad.

I was counting the money again to see if I could make it a bit more when I heard feet thudding up the stairs and Angela suddenly poked her head round my bedroom door.

"Your mum sent me up," she said. "What's up with you? You look as if you've just lost your best friend. Well, here I am, folks." And she came dancing sideways into the room kicking her legs high in the air like a chorus girl in a pantomime. And she had that soft black leather jacket on with matching gloves and black velvet trousers and new leather boots. She's got more nice clothes than Sindy doll.

"I'm a bit fed up," I admitted, starting to put the money into my purse. "It's my dad's birthday next week, and this all I've got to buy him a present with. Two pounds eighty-nine pence."

"It's not a lot," agreed Angela. "Tell you what, Charlie. Let's go shopping now. I'll help you choose something nice."

That cheered me up all right. Angela has a

knack for choosing just the right sort of present, and shopping with her is always fun. So I bundled myself into my big blue anorak with the spiky fur round the hood and put two pairs of thick woolly socks on under my wellies and pulled on my nice new sheepskin mittens that my Grandma sent me for Christmas. Angela started to giggle.

"You look like an Eskimo," she said, as we went down to the kitchen to tell my mum where we were going.

"Why don't you get the bus into Barlow?" suggested my mum, when I explained about the present. "There'll be more choice there. They've got a Boots and a Smiths."

Angela and I both thought that was a good idea, so off we went down the road to the bus stop.

On the way we passed the gate of number twenty-seven, where a new family had moved in just a few days before. Angela stopped suddenly and began to rummage in her pockets.

"Hang on a minute, Charlie," she said. "I've got to give a note to Mrs. Cart. From my mum." She fished a bit of paper from her jacket pocket.

"It's just a list of addresses and stuff. Doctors and dentists and things like that."

"I haven't met the new people yet," I said. "Are they nice?"

"Mr. Cart plays the buffoon in an orchestra," she said, opening the gate.

"I think you mean bassoon," I told her with a giggle.

"I thought it was the same thing," said Angela. "Oh, and Mrs. Cart breeds white pedigree cats." She looked at me and narrowed her eyes. "Tell you what, you can take the note in for me. Then you'll see them for yourself. Mrs. Cart might show you her six baby kittens."

"Kittens," I said. "Ooh, yes. I'll go. But why don't we go together?"

"She's more likely to ask you in if you're by yourself," said Angela. I started towards the front door, and then Angela suddenly seemed to remember something.

"You'll have to shout, Charlie," she said. "Mrs. Cart is as deaf as a dustbin."

"Must be from having to listen to all that buffoon-playing," I said, as I walked up the slippery path.

So I banged hard on the knocker and rang the bell six times to make sure Mrs. Cart heard me. I could see Angela peeping over the gate and grinning at me encouragingly. Then the door was opened by a very tall thin lady with grey hair all scraped back in a bun.

"Hello?" she said. "Yes?"

"I'm Charlie Ellis," I began. The lady looked a bit puzzled, and I thought she hadn't heard me. So I started again.

"I'M CHARLIE ELLIS," I shouted. "ANGELA MITCHELL'S FRIEND. MRS. MITCHELL SENT YOU THIS."

Mrs. Cart took the bit of paper. "Oh yes, thank you," she said. "That's very kind of you." A cold wind blew into the doorway and she shivered. "It's freezing out there," she said. "Would you like to come in and get warm for a minute?" And she led me into the hall.

She watched me stamp the snow off my wellies on the hall mat and then she led me into the big front room where a cosy log fire was burning. And on the rug in front of the fire was a basket, full of the loveliest white kittens you ever saw. They had long silky fur and big blue

eyes and the mother cat was licking them and
purring and looking ever so proud of herself.
I knelt down to stroke them and the mother
cat licked my hand with her warm rough
tongue.

"They're sweet, aren't they?" said Mrs. Cart
from the doorway.

"THEY'RE LOVELY," I bellowed loudly.
And you should have seen those poor kittens
scatter. They leapt out of the basket and shot
under the sofa, where they turned and peeped
out with round anxious eyes.

"Now look what you've done. You've frightened them," tutted Mrs. Cart, and she hurried
me out to the front door.

"GOODBYE, MRS. CART," I shouted.
"THANK YOU FOR SHOWING ME THE
CATS."

Mrs. Cart winced and put her hands over her
ears. "You don't have to shout like that, you
know," she said mildly. "I'm not deaf." And she
shut the door.

I stared at the door for a moment and then
turned away. I wasn't half embarrassed, I can tell
you. Whatever must she have thought of me?

I walked back down the path, wondering how Angela could have made such a mistake.

As soon as I saw her I knew. It wasn't a mistake at all. She was laughing her head off, holding her stomach and leaning weakly against the lamp post with her hanky stuffed in her mouth.

"Ha-ha! Very funny," I said furiously. "Mrs. Cart must think I'm a lunatic." And she started whooping and cackling all over again.

"GOODBYE, MRS. CART," she mimicked, at the top of her voice. And even though I was mad with her I still couldn't help seeing the funny side of it.

In no time at all I found myself giggling as much as she was. We giggled and slithered and clung together all the way to the bus stop, and even in the bus queue we kept bursting out into more giggles until everybody stared at us as if we were not all there. And when the bus came Angela paid my fare out of her own pocket money, which just goes to show how nice she can be when she wants to.

Anyway, we got to Barlow at last. We walked up and down that High Street in the cold for hours and hours and went into a hundred different shops, but still we couldn't find the right sort of present for my dad. We wandered around Boots and W. H. Smith and looked at books and pens and aftershave stuff and I couldn't see one single thing I thought he would like. We went into Mr. Chalk's and looked at garden stuff and tools but that was no good because I couldn't remember what things my dad already had. We were starting to get fed up with the whole thing, and even Angela seemed short of ideas.

And then, as we were walking past the window of the Barlow Wine Shop, Angela suddenly grabbed my arm.

"Charlie," she said breathlessly. "What is it that your dad likes better than anything?"

"Newcastle United football team," I said.

"Apart from that," she said impatiently. "What does he like to drink?"

"He likes a pint of beer now and again," I said slowly. "Oh, and he loves a glass of red wine with his dinner."

"Exactly," crowed Angela triumphantly. And she pointed to the shop window in front of me.

Right in the middle was a big display of French wines, and a card saying "For one week only. £2.85 per bottle." And in the very front of the display I could see a bottle of my dad's favourite wine.

"Wow," I said faintly. And I thought of my dad's delighted face when he opened it.

"That's it, Charlie," said Angela. "Come on." And she pulled me into the shop.

Behind the counter was an enormous whiskery man with a round face and a big red nose who looked as if he spent more time drinking the stuff than selling it. Angela explained what we wanted and I pointed out the right bottle in the window. But the man shook his head emphatically.

"Sorry," he said, and I could tell he wasn't really. "Can't sell alcohol to minors."

"We're not miners," said Angela indignantly, and I gave a snort of laughter at the thought of her digging coal.

"You're under age," said the fat man impatiently, pointing to a notice above the door. "I'll lose me licence if I break the law."

Angela and I turned round and read the

notice. It had a lot of hard words in it, but I could understand enough. The man was right. He wasn't allowed to sell wine to children, and I felt so disappointed I could have cried.

Angela wouldn't give up so easily. "It's for a present," she wheedled, batting her long eyelashes hopefully. "For her dad's birthday. We wouldn't tell a soul where we got it."

"No chance," replied the man flatly, folding his arms against his chest. "They all say that, sunshine."

"Let's go, Angela," I said, tugging her elbow. "It's no use." We trailed dismally out of the shop, and when we were safely outside Angela relieved her feelings by making rude faces and sticking her tongue out at the man through the window.

I dragged her away before she got us both into trouble. We started trudging back up the High Street, kicking moodily at lumps of frozen slush with our boots. It was so cold that our breath came out in little puffs of steam.

"I suppose I'd better settle for some aftershave or something," I sighed. "Let's go back to the chemist."

And it was when we were walking through Boots to the gifts counter that Angela had her fantastic idea.

"Charlie," she said excitedly, her eyes going all sparkly with delight. "I think I've just had a brainwave." And she picked up a large can off a nearby shelf and waved it under my nose.

"Concentrated grape juice?" I said, looking at the label. "Yuck. My dad won't like that."

She poked me in the ribs and went on grinning like a pillar box. "Read the rest, stupid," she urged.

I peered at the small print.

"Makes one gallon of rich, full-bodied red wine," I read aloud, suddenly feeling awestruck. "Just add water, sugar and yeast. Full instructions on back of label."

Angela did a little jig on the spot.

"It's even better than a bottle of wine," she said. "It makes a whole gallon. Imagine how pleased your dad will be with a *whole gallon* of red wine."

I didn't have any trouble imagining that. But I was a bit worried about actually making the stuff.

"It's difficult to make," I said doubtfully. "You need loads of equipment and stuff." I gazed round the other shelves in the section, full of things for the home wine-maker. Special containers, packets of this, jars of that. It all looked very complicated.

"You don't really need any of that rubbish," said Angela airily. "I know how to do it. My Uncle Peter is always making it, and he sometimes lets me help him. It's as easy as pie. Honest."

She sounded so confident that I believed her. And when I did some adding up in my head I found that the cost of the grape juice plus a little packet of special wine yeast came to two pounds seventy-nine pence. I made up my mind.

"All right," I said. "We'll get it. But it'll only leave me with ten pence left for my bus fare home."

"Don't worry about that," said Angela, giving me a quick hug. "And don't worry about the sugar, either. I'll pinch a bit from my mum's store cupboard."

I thought we might have trouble at the check-out because of being under age, but the cashier didn't bat an eyelid. She put the things in a bag and took our money in a bored sort of way, and I thought what a funny world it is that won't let children buy a bottle of wine but lets them buy enough stuff to make a whole gallon.

"How much wine is a gallon, anyway?" I said to Angela when we were safely outside.

"Six bottles," said Angela gleefully. And we danced hand in hand like little kids all the way up the road to the bus stop.

On the way home in the bus we made our plans.

"It's Scrabble night tonight," she reminded me. "And it's your mum's and dad's turn to come to our house. I'll come round as soon as they get started, to watch telly with you as usual. That'll give us plenty of time to make the wine."

I felt so pleased with the whole idea I could hardly wait for the evening to come. But I didn't feel quite so pleased when I got home and shut myself in my bedroom to read the label on the can.

I carefully peeled it off without tearing it so I could read the full instructions on the back. And it didn't look anything like as easy as Angela had made out. You needed a load of stuff we didn't have, like a gallon-sized glass jar for one thing, and a fermentation lock, whatever that was, for another. But that wasn't all. The worst thing was, even if you had all the right sort of equipment, the wine wouldn't be ready for three whole weeks. Far too late for my dad's birthday.

I started on her the minute she came in the back door at seven o'clock that evening.

"It's not going to work," I said. "We haven't got a . . ." My voice tailed off when I saw that she was staggering under the weight of an enormous glass jar.

"It's an old cider jar," she said, looking pleased with herself. "It holds a gallon. It's been in the cupboard under the stairs for years." She stood it on the kitchen table and blew some dust off the top. "Look, it's even got a proper screw-on cap."

"We need a lock," I said. "A fermentation lock. It says so on the label."

Angela shook her head. "This is just as good, I'm sure," she said. "A fermentation lock only locks in the fermentation. If we screw the cap on really tight it'll be OK."

She looked at me closely.

"What's up, Charlie?" she said. "You look fed up. I thought you liked the idea."

"I did," I said gloomily. "But the wine isn't going to be ready in time for my dad's birthday. It takes three weeks to ferment." And I waved the instruction label under her nose.

Angela's face fell. "Are you sure?" she said. "Bloomin' heck, I never thought of that." She read the label carefully, and then started pacing up and down the kitchen floor. You could almost hear her brain tick.

She suddenly turned to face me and her whole face had brightened up.

"Listen, Charlie," she said. "What is it that makes the wine ferment?"

I gazed at her blankly. "Well . . . er . . . the yeast, I suppose," I said. I picked up the label and had another look. "Yes, look. It says 'One teaspoon of yeast will ferment one gallon of wine in three weeks'." Angela stared hard into my eyes.

"So how long will it take *three* teaspoons of yeast?" she said softly.

I frowned helplessly at the ceiling. I hate those sums that are all about seven and a half men taking three and a quarter hours to mow five and three-quarter acres of grass and how long would it take a hundred and twenty men to mow twice as much. But I managed to work it out in the end.

"One week," I said at last, grinning all over my face. And Angela whistled and stamped and applauded me as if I had won a gold medal.

And so that's how we did it. We mixed the grape juice with ten ounces of sugar from Auntie Sally's store cupboard and poured it all into the cider jar. We filled it almost to the top with warm water and then added three heaped spoonfuls of yeast.

"Put another one in," said Angela. "Just to make sure."

So I added another spoonful and Angela screwed down the cap as hard as she could to lock in the fermentation.

"Where's the warmest place in the house?" she said, when we had finished. "It's got to be kept nice and warm."

"The airing cupboard," I said at once. "The central heating boiler's in there. And it's on all the time in this cold weather."

So we lugged the heavy jar between us up the stairs and heaved it into the back of the airing cupboard in the bathroom. And we piled up all my mum's clean sheets and towels and pillow-cases in front of it so that nobody would know it was there.

"Why is the stuff fizzing like that?" I said, as we shut the airing cupboard door. "Are you sure it's all right?"

"All the best wines are fizzy," said Angela, tossing her curls. "Think of champagne." And I had to admit she was right.

Three nights later it happened. My dad had been working late and my mum let me stay up to have supper with them and the three of us were sitting round the kitchen table eating chicken and mushroom pie and mashed potatoes and peas.

"I met the new family down the street today," my mum was saying, passing my dad the salt and pepper. "Mr. and Mrs. Cart. They seem very pleasant." My dad winked at me.

"They've got a son called Orson," he said innocently.

"Really?" said my mum. "Orson Cart?" And I laughed so much I almost choked.

"Honestly, Ted," tutted my mum, handing me a glass of water. And that's when we heard the most almighty explosion right above our heads.

And in no time at all it was pandemonium with my mum screaming that the bomb had dropped and she had known it was going to happen and my dad leaping up and knocking over his chair and shouting about a gas explosion and the central heating boiler and the house going up in flames any minute now. And he bundled us both out of the front door into the freezing cold black night and my mum went twittering on about her jewellery and her fur coat but my dad took no notice and went haring off to warn the Mitchells and phone the gas board and the fire brigade leaving us standing in the street gazing fearfully at the house windows and expecting flames to appear at any moment.

"Wow, isn't it exciting?" hissed a voice into my ear. And there was Angela, huddled up in a great big blanket over her pyjamas because she had been just on her way to bed. Then Uncle Jim and Auntie Sally arrived, and several other neighbours came out to see what was going on, and everybody kept asking everybody else what had happened and nobody seemed to know.

I said nothing. I had a very funny feeling in my bones.

Well, finally the fire brigade arrived with a great big fire engine and fireproof suits and gas masks and enormous great hoses expecting to find the whole street ablaze. And all they found when they went bravely into the house was one shattered glass jar and an airing cupboard full of wine-soaked sheets and a horrible boozy smell like the back door of a pub.

And of course it was me that got the blame. All the grownups looked so grim that I could hardly speak, but I managed to blurt it all out somehow. And while I was telling them how it all happened, I very nearly burst into tears.

I was upset about my mum's best embroidered sheets that she'd had as a wedding present and would never be the same again. I was upset about all the trouble I'd caused for everybody, especially that young ginger-haired fireman who kept scowling at me as if I'd blown up the place on purpose.

But most of all I was upset about my dad. I had been looking forward so much to seeing his delighted face when I gave him six whole bottles of wine for his birthday, and now I had nothing to give him at all. I wished I had never set eyes on that Angela Mitchell and her rotten ideas.

Well, I stood there sniffing and hiccupping and wiping my eyes on the sleeve of my Snoopy sweatshirt, feeling miserable and sorry for myself, and all of a sudden Angela did a most astonishing thing. She came forward and put her arms tight round my shoulders, and she looked as if she was about to cry, too.

"It wasn't Charlie's fault," she gulped loudly, and everybody stopped arguing about it and turned round to stare at her. "The whole thing was my idea," she went on defiantly. "So if anybody's going to get into trouble it should be me."

And in the end neither of us got into trouble. I think they were all so totally amazed at Angela taking the blame for once that nobody had the heart to get really cross.

I was pretty amazed myself, I can tell you. It just goes to show, with a girl like her you simply never know where you are.

Chapter Four

I always look forward to the times when my grandma comes to stay. She's my dad's mum and she comes from a little fishing village in Northumberland, and she's small and round and cuddly. You should hear the lovely funny way she talks. Sometimes you can't understand what she's talking about, and my dad has to translate. And when she's here for a holiday she never stops cooking from the minute she arrives until the minute she leaves because she's convinced that my dad and I don't get enough to eat.

"Ee, hinny," she says, poking me in the ribs. "There's not a scrap of meat on them bones of yours. We'll soon fettle that." And she rolls her sleeves up and puts a pinny on and sets to work baking scones and stotty cakes and the yummiest minced beef and potato pies you ever tasted. And my dad has the time of his life, until Grandma goes home again and he has to go straight back on his diet.

One Saturday morning during the Easter holidays my mum was out shopping and my dad was at the barber's getting his hair cut, what there is left of it, that is. And my grandma and I were having a great old time rolling out pastry and baking apple turnovers and jam tarts and stuff. I was glad to be indoors in our nice cosy kitchen on such a nasty cold day, especially with my grandma for company. She was cutting out the circles of dough and I was putting them in the tray and spooning dollops of jam into them. Quite a lot of the jam was finding its way into my mouth.

"Give over, our Charlie," said my grandma, rapping my knuckles with a wooden spoon. "You'll not want any dinner. And then it'll be me gets the blame from your mam."

Just then there was a loud bang at the back door and Angela stuck her head in.

"Hi, Charlie," she said. "Hi, Mrs. Ellis. Coo, it's lovely and warm in here."

Angela came in and shut the door. "It's freezing out there. What shall we do, Charlie?"

I scowled at her, not feeling pleased to see her at all. I was quite happy as I was. But she had come round specially to see me and I supposed I could hardly just tell her to go away. My grandma could though. She's never been all that fond of Angela.

"You can both get away upstairs out of my way," she said, shooing Angela and me out of the kitchen.

"Let's play in your room," said Angela. So we went upstairs.

Angela had brought her new radio cassette player with her, and as soon as we were in my room she switched it on.

"We don't need the radio on," I said. "Come on, we'll have a game of draughts." And I started to pull the board and the box of draughts from under my bed. I like playing draughts with Angela because I usually win. It's the only game she hasn't worked out a way of cheating at.

"We can listen while we play," she said. "This is ever such a good programme, Charlie. It's a new local radio station."

So we set up the draughts while the radio churned out pop music. I was just starting to get interested in the game when Angela suddenly leaned over and turned up the volume.

"What was that?" she said. "Listen. They're talking about our village."

The voice sounded strangely familiar, in spite of the vague American accent that all disc jockeys and telly announcers seem to have these days, but what really made my ears prick up was the word cheeseburger. Cheeseburgers are one of the things I love best in the whole world.

". . . to celebrate the thirtieth anniversary of our international hamburger company," the voice was saying. "Don't miss this opportunity. Sample our new giant MacDougal Cheeseburger. Entirely free of charge. In the following MacDougal branches today. Thames Street, Cookburn. The Parade, Edgebourne. And West Street, Barlow. Taste a free MacDougal Cheeseburger TODAY!"

There was a sort of click and a crackle and then more music. I stared at Angela and Angela stared at me. The draught board lay forgotten between us.

"Charlie," she said slowly. "Did you hear what I heard? Free giant cheeseburgers? The Parade, Edgebourne. Wowee!"

I could almost taste those onions already. "Come on, Angela," I said. "We can be there in two minutes."

We tumbled helter-skelter down the stairs and out of the back door, shouting "'Bye, back in a minute," to my astonished grandma as we went.

We reached our gate and Angela, instead of coming with me, turned towards her own house.

"I'd better just pop home and tell my mum where I'm going," she said. "You run ahead and get a place in the queue. There's bound to be thousands of people."

So I tore off along the street as fast as I could go, and I was in such a hurry that I didn't look where I was going and collided with Miss Menzies coming out of her gate. Miss Menzies is the fattest person I know, and it knocked the wind clean out of me, I can tell you. It was a bit like colliding with an elephant.

"Charlie," gasped Miss Menzies, going as red as her knitted woolly hat. "What's all the hurry?"

"Sorry," I said hastily, trying to get my breath back. "I'm in a bit of a hurry. They're giving away free cheeseburgers at MacDougals in the Parade."

"They're what?" squealed Miss Menzies, her little piggy eyes lighting up greedily. "Are you sure?"

"It's just been on the radio," I said. And I set off again with Miss Menzies lumbering along behind me, all her rolls of fat wobbling with the effort. It's amazing how fast fat people can run when there's free food at the end of it.

I reached the High Street and ran past the paper shop, and who should be coming out but that fat fool Laurence Parker and that nice David Watkins who's going to be an astronaut when he grows up. Remember that story about Henny Penny running around telling everybody the news when the sky fell on her head? Well, that's just how I felt, puffing out the story of the free cheeseburgers all over again, while the two of them stood there with their mouths open.

"Garn. You're having us on," jeered Laurence Parker. "Free cheeseburgers. What a load of cogglewoggle." He took David's arm. "Come on,

Dave. She's pulling a fast one. You know what she's like, her and that Angela Mitchell."

"It's true," I insisted, feeling hurt. "Honest. Cross my heart. It was on the radio, only five minutes ago."

The two boys stared at me for a moment.

"It won't do any harm to go and look," said David at last.

"All right," said Laurence. "But I'm warning you, Charlie Ellis. If this is a hoax, you're not half in for it."

Miss Menzies had just about caught up by now, and the four of us hurried round the corner into the Parade, expecting to find an enormous crowd outside MacDougal's.

There was nobody there. We all stood outside, peering stupidly in through the window and gasping and panting for breath. Two elderly ladies drinking tea stared back in surprise. And two youths in motorcycle jackets and boots stopped eating their sausage, egg and beans and made rude signs at us through the glass.

"It was on the radio," I said helplessly. "Angela heard it too. It was her radio," I added, as if that made the slightest bit of difference.

"Well, there's no point in standing out here," said Laurence Parker sensibly. "Let's go in and ask."

So we all trooped in and went up to the counter where a chef with a black droopy moustache and a white apron and a tall white hat was sharpening a long steel knife. He opened his mouth wide and hooted with laughter when I asked in a small voice about free cheeseburgers and I could see all the fillings in his teeth.

"Nar. There's nothing like that happening around here. MacDougal's never give nothing away, far as I know." He called over to the waitress, busily wiping tables in the corner. "You know anything about it, Betty?" The waitress shook her head.

"Somebody having you on, I expect," said the chef. "But I can soon rustle you up a few cheeseburgers, if that's what you're after. One pound ninety-five pence each."

Nobody had any money and we all shuffled out, red in the face. Miss Menzies looked as if she was about to cry. And I don't know what Laurence Parker would have done to me if my dad hadn't come out of the barber's shop just at that moment.

"Dad!" I shouted, and flung myself at him. I've never been so pleased to see him in my life.

"Charlie," he said, looking cross. "What are you doing? Out in the cold with no coat on? I thought you were at home helping Grandma."

And so I had to tell the whole story all over again, with the others standing around butting in now and again with rude remarks.

"And now nobody believes me," I said helplessly. "But it *was* on the radio. Cross my heart."

My dad scratched his head and looked baffled. "You must have made a mistake, pet. Perhaps you got the day wrong or something."

"That's all very well," grumbled Miss Menzies. "But she's made me run all this way for nothing."

Laurence Parker and David Watkins marched away up the street making disgusted faces. My dad smiled at Miss Menzies soothingly.

"Come on," he said. "I'll buy you a cheeseburger. The biggest one they've got." And Miss Menzies brightened up at once.

Well, of course by then I was so upset I couldn't have eaten a cheeseburger to save my life. So we left Miss Menzies happily tucking in and set off home, expecting to meet Angela on the way back.

"I can't understand it," I said. "She only went to tell her mum where we were going. She should have caught up by now."

My dad made a grim face and shook his head. "It all sounds a bit fishy to me," he said. "I still reckon it's one of her tricks. And I wouldn't mind having a look at that radio of hers," he added, as we went in the back door.

So while my dad was telling my grandma all about it, I ran upstairs to my room. I picked up the radio and carried it down to the kitchen.

"It's still switched on," I said to my dad. "But it's making ever such a funny noise. A sort of whispery, scratchy noise." My dad took it from me and pressed some of the switches.

"Just as I thought," he said. "Listen to this Charlie. It's not the radio at all. It's a tape."

He pushed the rewind button and the tape whizzed back to the beginning. And my mouth fell open as the same pop music I'd heard earlier filled the kitchen. Then a sudden click, a crackle, and a voice.

"Hurry, all you Edgebourne cheeseburger fans.

Try a free giant MacDougal cheeseburger today. To celebrate the thirtieth anniversary of our international hamburger company. Don't miss this opportunity . . ."

My dad switched off the tape and the three of us sat down at the kitchen table looking glum. There was a long silence.

"It was Angela's Uncle Peter's voice," I said weakly. "I recognise it now. She must have got him to help her. I bet they're both laughing their socks off by now."

"Well, what a nasty trick to play on a friend," said my grandma, pursing her lips. "That Angela wants her behind tanned, if you ask me." Then a sudden gleam came into her blue eyes and she jumped to her feet.

"We'll fettle them," she grinned, fastening her pinny more firmly round her waist and pushing a stray wisp of white hair out of her eyes. "Cheeseburger, was it? I'll show 'em cheeseburger." And my dad and I watched in astonishment as she banged the frying pan on the stove and went into action.

She put four beefburgers and some chopped onion in the frying pan and while they were sizzling away she cut open a whole stotty cake. And if you've never seen a stotty cake it's a sort of flat round bread roll about the size of a dinner plate. My grandma spread the stotty cake with butter, then put the slices of cheese on it and popped it under the grill to brown. When the cheese was all bubbly she crammed the four beef-burgers together on one half of the stotty cake and plonked the other half triumphantly on top.

"There," she said, her face all pink. "Show that to your fine friends next door."

I looked at it and giggled. It was the biggest cheeseburger in the world, and I couldn't wait to see Angela's face. I put on my anorak and my woolly hat, hung Angela's radio by its strap on my shoulder, and picked up the enormous cheeseburger.

It was so big it took two hands to hold it. My dad had to open the door for me to let me out, and my grandma was laughing so much she had to keep wiping her eyes on her apron.

Anyway, I strolled round the corner and sauntered into Angela's drive. I stood leaning against the gate where I knew I could be seen from the windows, and I started taking great bites out of that cheeseburger.

"Yum, yum," I kept saying loudly, and it wasn't long before a face appeared at the window. Angela's Uncle Peter. And his eyes bulged out of his head when he saw what I was eating.

Then the back door opened and Angela came rushing out.

"Flippin' heck," she said. "Where did you get that?"

"Um . . . yum . . . er . . . I brought your radio back," I said, with my mouth full. I waved the cheeseburger under her nose so she could smell those onions and that lovely toasted cheese. "Best cheeseburger I ever tasted," I said, taking another huge bite and licking melted butter off my wrist. "Pity you didn't get there in time."

Angela looked so flabbergasted I almost choked. She hung on the gate beside me and watched enviously.

"Go on, Charlie. Give me a bit," she wheedled. "You're never going to manage all that by yourself."

I don't know how I did it but I did. I ate it all. Every scrap. Right down to the last bite. And I didn't give her one single crumb. I was so full I almost burst, but it was worth it just to see her face.

Chapter Five

IT was one of those hot, lazy, summer days when all you want to do is lie on your back among the buttercups and listen to the bees buzzing by. Being stuck in a classroom felt like being in prison, and I couldn't wait for the afternoon to end.

Miss March was giving us an English lesson. It was all about the meaning of words. She would call out a word and we all had to write down a sentence with that word in it. It was too easy, and I was almost dozing off.

"Ready, everyone?" said Miss March, looking as bored as I felt. "The next word is BENIGN."

This was a bit more interesting. I thought for a moment and then wrote 'The generous king was kind and benign to his people.'

I was pleased with what I had written and was one of the first to put up my hand. But Miss March didn't pick me to read it out. Angela had her hand up, too, and Miss March picked her.

Angela got to her feet, her exercise book in her hand. She cleared her throat importantly.

"My cousin is eight years old but he'll be nine next week," she read out, scowling ferociously when everybody began to snigger. And then her face went pink when Miss March stood up and wrote BENIGN on the blackboard in big capital letters.

"Oh," said Angela lamely. "I thought you meant . . ."

"You'd better learn that word thoroughly, Angela," interrupted Miss March severely. "It could well crop up in your spelling test tomorrow. And I hope you're going to do better than last week, otherwise you and I are going to fall out."

Angela cowered. Falling out with Miss March is a bit like falling out with a grizzly bear. There's no way you could call it a fair fight.

"It's all right for you," she grumbled as we walked home together after school. "You'll get

twenty out of twenty as usual. Plus a gold star.
Plus the spelling cup for yet another week
running." She kicked a dandelion clock clean off
its stalk with the toe of her sandal and I watched
the fluffy seeds float away into the air.

Angela hates spelling because she's so hopeless
at it. She gets dead cross with me for winning the
spelling cup practically every week, but I can't
help it if I'm a good speller, can I?

"I'll get six out of twenty and a good telling
off, more than likely," she said gloomily, stalk-
ing off down the road. I ran to catch her up.

"Listen, Angela," I said. "I could help you to
learn the words. It's not hard really. You just
have to work at it a bit."

Angela shook her head. "It wouldn't be any
use," she said. "I'd only forget them by tomorrow.
In any case," she added peevishly, "there's never
any hope of beating you, is there?"

She hurried on, her shoulders hunched
dejectedly. I trotted along beside her, wondering
what I could do to cheer her up. I hate it when
she's miserable. It makes me miserable, too.

I decided to try a funny poem. "There was a
young lady called Vickers," I began.

"You've told me that one," she said wearily. "And anyway, it's rude. My mum said so."

I racked my brains and tried again. "What did the honey bee say when it came back from its holidays? There's no place like comb. *Comb*. Get it?"

She took no notice. It was like talking to a tree. Then suddenly she turned to me.

"Are you really my friend, Charlie Ellis?" she demanded.

"Er . . . yes," I said. "Of course I am. Why?" And my heart sank as I wondered how I was supposed to prove it this time.

"Suppose we both pretended to feel ill tomorrow morning," she said, her face lighting up as the idea took shape. "We could have a day off school. We'd miss the rotten old spelling test for once. And we could lie in the sun all day on your dad's new patio."

"But I don't want to miss the spelling test," I objected. "I've worked hard all week and I know the words off by heart. If I don't go to school that awful Delilah Jones will get the cup . . ."

My voice faltered because she was looking daggers at me. "But you take the day off if you want," I added hastily. "It's a good idea."

"It wouldn't be any fun on my own," said Angela coldly. "And you know it. But I might have known it would be no use asking you to do anything for me. All you think about is yourself." And she went marching off, her head in the air.

I stood there for a while, thinking about what she had said. Maybe I was being a bit selfish. There couldn't be much harm in taking a day off school, after all. We wouldn't be getting anybody into trouble. And I had to admit that I quite fancied the idea of a day in the sunshine on my dad's nice new patio. I made up my mind.

"Angela," I called after her, and she turned round, her face starting to glow the way it does when she gets her own way.

And so we made our plans, walking along arm in arm with our heads close together. It would have to be a tummy bug, Angela said, and we could start tonight by running backwards and forwards to the loo all evening and pretending to flush the toilet every half hour or so. Then a pain in the stomach tomorrow morning would seem a lot more convincing.

"And it's not going to be at all suspicious that we've both got it," said Angela. "After all, we do everything together, don't we?"

Angela was by now in the best of moods, giggling and joking as we strolled through the village. So I wasn't at all prepared for her next piece of mischief.

We were walking past Harris and Deans, the estate agents, when she was attracted by a notice in the window. 'Let us sell your house,' it said, in blue and gold letters at least a foot high. "Speed and Efficiency is our motto. Surveyor's valuation free."

Angela's blue eyes turned green and narrow like a cat's.

"Hang on, Charlie," she said. "We'll just pop in here." She pulled me up the two polished marble steps and through the glass swing doors. An elegant young lady with jewelled spectacles and purple painted fingernails tapped at a typewriter in a posh reception area with black leather chairs and deep blue carpet.

"May I help you?" she enquired haughtily, looking us up and down and not seeming too impressed with what she saw.

"Oh, good afternoon," said Angela, equally haughtily. "My parents asked me to call as I was passing, as our telephone is unfortunately out of order. We are thinking of selling the house and we wondered whether you'd care to handle the sale. We live in Bishopsbrook Road."

The receptionist stood up. "I'll see if Mr. Harris can help," she said politely, and walked through a green door into an inner office.

"I didn't know you were moving," I hissed into Angela's ear, as soon as we were alone.

"We're not," she hissed back, squeezing my hand and starting to giggle at my puzzled face.

A tall, thin young man in a smart grey suit and a pink and white striped shirt hurried in. He didn't look a bit startled to see a couple of kids like us, so the secretary must have explained.

"Good afternoon," he said, waving us towards the posh leather seats. "I understand your parents would like me to call and give a valuation? I could probably manage tomorrow if that would be convenient? Fine. If you could just write the name and address on this form. I would of course normally ring for an appointment, but I gather your telephone is out of order?"

"Yes. Such a nuisance," murmured Angela. She scribbled quickly on the form, handed it back and made polite goodbyes.

As soon as we got outside she began to race along the High Street, whooping and laughing and throwing her satchel in the air. I followed more slowly, trying hard to work it out. What I couldn't understand was, how did she think she could get away with a trick like that? When the estate agent called the next day, he would find out it was all a hoax. And Angela would have to take the blame. I was baffled by the whole thing.

"Don't fuss, Charlie," she said, when I begged her to explain. "You sound just like your mother."

Anyway, we parted the best of friends, promising to see each other the next day. And all that evening I pretended to be feeling a bit off colour. It was very hard to leave my supper of fried chicken and chips and raspberry flan and cream, but I knew I had to, if the plan was to work. So I just picked at it a bit and heaved big sighs, and then I suddenly rushed off to the bathroom. I made sure I flushed the loo as noisily as I could, and when I came back to the table my mum and dad were both looking concerned.

"Are you feeling all right, bonny lass?" my dad said, putting his hand on my forehead. "She feels a bit hot," he told my mum. "Bit of a temperature, I think."

And I was rather hot, I can tell you. It felt awful to be fooling my mum and dad like this, and when I saw how anxious they both were my face went even redder.

"I . . . er . . . I think I've got an upset tummy," I stammered out. "The meat tasted a bit funny today."

"Bed for you, young lady," said my mum decisively, picking up my plate and scraping my chicken and chips into the pedal bin and tapping Daniel on the nose to stop him diving in after it.

"What, now?" I said, horrified. "But it's only seven o'clock. I'll miss Top of the Pops on the telly. Aw, mum, I can't miss Top of the Pops."

"Bed," said my mum. "Top of the Pops is a load of rubbish, anyway. It won't do you any harm to miss it for once."

I knew it was no use arguing, so I contented myself with a few rude words under my breath. Off I went and got into my pyjamas and climbed into bed. And I had to lie there and waste all that lovely summer evening while the breeze ruffled the curtains through the open window and a thrush sang in the apple tree just outside. And I had to swallow a great big tablespoonful of horrible, nasty, smelly, chalky stuff which was supposed to make me feel better but nearly made me puke up all over the nice pink quilt. I was bored and fed up and lonely because my mum wouldn't even let me have Daniel in my room. It seemed like the longest evening of my life, but at last I suppose I must have fallen asleep.

The first thing I remembered when I woke up the next morning was Angela's plan. So I crept downstairs before anybody else was up to get some flour to rub on my cheeks.

"Sssh!" I hissed at Daniel, who leapt out of his basket when he saw me and started rolling about on the lino wanting his stomach scratched. "Basket!" He gave me a sorrowful look, but he did go back at last, so I quickly dabbed on the flour and crept back to my room. I still looked far too healthy so I used a bit of grey watercolour paint to make dark smudges under my eyes, being careful not to overdo it and spoil the whole thing. As soon as I heard somebody getting up

and moving about I locked myself in the bathroom and made loud retching noises for a while.
When I came out clutching my tummy I found
my dad waiting on the landing.

"Still a bit queasy, are you, pet?" he said
sympathetically. Then he noticed my face.
"Good lord, you look awful. I'd hop back into
bed if I were you. There'll be no school for you
today."

I could hear them in their bedroom arguing
about whether to call the doctor or not, and I
wasn't half glad when they decided not to.

"It's only a bit of a bug, I expect," said my
dad. "Let her have the day off school and keep
an eye on her. I'll take her along to the surgery if
she's not better by this evening."

"I've got a hair appointment this morning,"
said my mum. "I'd better cancel it, I suppose."

My dad wouldn't hear of it. "Don't spoil your
plans, love," he said. "Tell you what, I'll phone
the office and tell them I'm not coming in. They
owe me a day off after all that overtime. I'll look
after Charlie and do a bit of gardening. OK?"

"All right," said my mum. "I might as well
make a day of it, in that case. Take Sally out for

lunch or something. We haven't had a day in town for ages."

I bounced gleefully about in bed when I heard that. I was glad my dad would be looking after me because I knew he wouldn't make me stay in bed all day. Angela and I could lie on the patio in the sun, just as we had planned. Daniel came suddenly bounding in and jumped on top of me and we bounced about together for a while, but then we both lay down quickly when my mum came in with the breakfast tray.

"Out," she said sternly to Daniel, and he slunk out of the door with his tail between his legs, and I don't think it's fair that dogs are not allowed on beds. When I grow up I'm going to have six dogs and I'm going to buy the biggest bed I can find so that they can all sleep on it with me. And if my husband doesn't like it he can sleep in another room.

Anyway, I sat up in bed and eagerly took my breakfast tray. After no supper last night I was ravenous, so you can imagine my disgust when I saw what my mum had brought. Two small slices of dry toast and a cup of tea with no milk or sugar. Yuck.

After a while my mum went off for her day out with Auntie Sally. I heard her in the hall, leaving strict instructions with my dad about my medicine, and not letting the dog on the bed, and then just as she was leaving she remembered something else.

"Oh, and there's a chance the man from Shortbridge's might call this afternoon," she said. "To measure up the sitting room for the new carpet. Get him to give you a rough idea of the cost, will you, dear?"

"Leave everything to me," my dad said.

The front door banged and all was quiet for a while. I snuggled down in bed with *The Wind in the Willows*, but I couldn't concentrate on reading. I kept expecting Angela to arrive at any second, because I knew Auntie Sally wouldn't leave her in the house on her own. She would send her round here so my dad could keep an eye on us both at the same time.

Eleven o'clock came, and there was still no Angela. My stomach had been rumbling like a steam roller for hours, so I got up, washed and dressed in shorts and a teeshirt, and went downstairs.

Daniel was so pleased to be let out of the kitchen that he almost knocked me over with his welcome. We went outside together and found my dad peacefully hoeing the potato patch in the sunshine.

"Hello, pet lamb," he said, smiling and leaning on his hoe. "I see you're feeling better."

"I'm not half hungry," I said. "I could eat a rhinoceros."

"I bet you could," said my dad. "But I think something a bit lighter would be better at the moment. Come on, let's see what we can find."

I sat at the kitchen table munching sugarpuffs while my dad made the lightest, fluffiest, most delicious mushroom omelette you ever saw. I had four slices of hot, buttered toast with it and a big mug of sweet, milky coffee. My dad sat at the other side of the table, drinking coffee and watching me eat, and I could see how pleased he was that I was better. It didn't half make me feel guilty, I can tell you.

Well, I waited all day and Angela never came. I hung about, feeling bored and not knowing what to do with myself, and the time went ever so slowly. I couldn't think what had happened to

Angela. Maybe she had overdone the symptoms and had been kept in bed.

My dad made some chicken sandwiches for lunch from the cold chicken from the night before, and we were just settling down on the patio to eat it when the doorbell rang.

"That'll be Angela," I said, jumping up quickly. And I could have bitten my tongue out because of course Angela was supposed to be at school and my dad gave me such a funny look.

Anyway, it wasn't Angela. It was the tall, thin man from the estate agent's, and he had a measuring tape and a clipboard in his hand.

"Hello again," he said, smiling.

I stared at him in surprise. And then all of a sudden it started to sink in. Angela had put down my name and address instead of hers. And my blood boiled when I realised that the whole thing was just a plot to get me into trouble.

"Good morning, Mr. Ellis," said the estate agent to my dad. "I'm Mr. Harris from . . ."

"Come in, come in," my dad interrupted cheerfully. "My wife said you might call. Just carry on and measure up. The sitting room's through there." And Mr. Harris went bustling off with his tape measure while my dad and I went back to our lunch.

I didn't know what to do. I couldn't let my dad know what was going on without telling tales on Angela. And where was Angela, anyway? I'd kill her when I got my hands on her, I promised myself.

We could see Mr. Harris measuring the kitchen now, and my dad stared at him through the window, his mouth open in surprise.

"All right if I go upstairs?" asked Mr. Harris, popping his head out of the kitchen door. "Three bedrooms, isn't it?"

"Go ahead," said my dad faintly, leaning back in his chair and turning a bit pale. "Your mother didn't tell me she was re-carpeting the whole darned house," he hissed at me when the man had gone.

I didn't say a word. We sat there together listening to Mr. Harris clumping about upstairs, and after a while he reappeared in the kitchen doorway.

"Tiled bathroom, three bedrooms," he was muttering to himself, writing busily on his clipboard. "Nice patio you've got, too. I'll just measure the garage, if I may?"

"The garage?" squeaked my dad, his voice coming out all funny and his eyebrows disappearing into his hair. "Did you say the garage?"

"Yes. And the garden too, while I'm out here," said Mr. Harris.

My dad watched in disbelief as the man stalked backwards and forwards between the fences with his tape measure.

"The man's mad," he said. "Stark raving bonkers. Who'd want to carpet the garden?" And even though I felt sure the whole story was going to have to come out any minute now, I still had to put my hand over my mouth to stop myself from bursting into giggles.

My dad was beginning to give me some very funny looks.

"There's something going on, isn't there," he said. "I'm not stupid. I'm going to find out just what he's up to." And he jumped up out of his chair. This is it, I thought, wondering whether I'd be sent to bed for a whole week this time.

Mr. Harris had finished measuring and was coming towards us. He shook my dad's hand.

"I'll be off now, Mr. Ellis," he said. "You'll be hearing from us in a few days."

"Look here," said my dad, getting a bit red in the face. "I don't think . . ."

"Don't worry," said Mr. Harris soothingly. "There's no obligation, you know. You're entirely free to change your mind, after we've discussed the price."

He walked through the house to the front door, scribbling on his clipboard and consulting his notes.

"We'll be sending you a written estimate, of course," he said. "But I think I can safely say it'll be around sixty-eight thousand pounds. Possibly a bit more. Goodbye, Mr. Ellis." And off he went down the drive.

My dad slumped against the doorpost, watching him go. He looked as if he'd been hit on the head with a sledge hammer. And I know I shouldn't laugh at my dad but this time he looked so funny I couldn't help it. I dashed upstairs to my room and shoved my head under the quilt and laughed until I choked.

Anyway, Angela's plan to get me into trouble hadn't worked, and I was dying to tell her so.

And she finally did turn up at last, just after four o'clock. I was lying on a rug on the patio with Daniel sprawled over my legs when I suddenly heard voices in the kitchen.

There was my mum, all smart and pretty with her new hairdo. And there was Auntie Sally, with her usual pile of boxes and carrier bags full of shopping. And neither of them took the slightest bit of notice of me when I went in. They were both cooing and fussing over a radiant, smiling Angela, who'd met them in the street *on her way home from school.*

"She really does deserve it, though," Auntie Sally was saying, gazing fondly at her daughter. "I've never seen her work so hard over her spellings. She was up practically all night."

Angela looked at me, her blue eyes dancing.

"Hi, Charlie," she said. "I hear you've got a tummy bug. What a shame you missed the test. Guess what? I won the spelling cup." And she held it up for me to see.

I don't know how I stopped myself from bashing her over the head with it. She really is a sly cat sometimes.

Chapter Six

IT takes some doing to play a trick on the whole class at the same time, but Angela managed to think of a way. And of course once again it was me that got the blame.

She worked herself up into a right old temper that day, and it was only because everybody laughed at her during the art lesson. Angela hates art anyway, and Miss March is always telling her off for messy, untidy work.

It was an interesting sort of lesson, because for a change we weren't doing painting. We were learning how to do that old-fashioned italic writing. And we all had those special pens with thick nibs and little bottles of black Indian ink.

We had to copy a poem from the blackboard, and I was quite enjoying making the nice curved shapes of the letters and putting fancy squiggly bits on the capitals. I only made one or two small blots, and on the whole I thought my effort wasn't too bad.

Angela, in the desk behind mine, wasn't getting on well at all. Everybody was working away quietly, with Miss March walking around the class looking over our shoulders and helping here and there, so we could all hear Angela sighing and moaning and screwing up her sheet of paper to start again.

"This is murder," she hissed in my ear. "This lousy pen doesn't work. It keeps making blobs."

"Try a new nib," I whispered, starting on the last line of the verse.

Angela clattered out to the front of the class to change her nib from the box on the shelf. When she got back to her place with a fresh piece of paper she found Miss March looming over her like a mountain.

"Angela Mitchell," said Miss March grimly. "I can't believe you haven't even started yet. Your paper's still blank. What have you been doing all this time?"

"She's been writing blank verse, Miss," said that cleverclogs Laurence Parker. "Like Shakespeare." And you should have heard the groans from the rest of the class.

"You've only got five minutes left, Angela," went on Miss March coldly, ignoring Laurence's remark. "If it's not finished by the end of the lesson you'll have to stay in after lunch. Now please get on with it."

I hoped Miss March might say something nice about my work on the way past, but she only gave it a quick glance and a nod and walked on. I finished the poem and put a neat little row of dots at the bottom. I blotted the ink carefully with a clean piece of blotting paper, then I looked over my shoulder at Angela.

She was scribbling away like a maniac, her face all red and her fingers smudged with ink. Her paper was a mess, all covered in splashes and dribbles and blotches, and she kept jabbing the pen furiously into the ink bottle as if she was trying to stab it to death.

The bell went for lunch and Angela finished just in time. She slumped back in her seat and flung down the pen with a huge sigh.

Miss March came to have a look. She picked up Angela's paper and glared at it in silence for a while. Angela didn't even look at her. She sank down in her chair, her eyes fixed on the desk.

"A five-year-old could have done better than this," said Miss March finally in a grim sort of voice. "It looks as if ten drunken spiders fell in the ink and crawled all over the page." And of course that's when the whole class fell about laughing. Not because it was all that funny, but because it was a teacher's joke.

Laurence Parker got the job of collecting all the papers and everybody else trooped out down the corridor.

"Never mind," I said to Angela, giving her arm a squeeze. "At least Miss Quick March didn't keep you in." But Angela was hardly listening. She had a very funny look in her eyes.

"They didn't have to laugh at me like that," she said moodily. "I'll think of a way to get even with the whole stupid lot of them. You'll see."

And all the time we were eating our school dinner in the dining hall Angela sat like a statue staring into space. She hardly ate any of her stew and carrots and mashed potatoes, or her apple crumble and custard, much to the delight of Laurence Parker, who scoffed the lot.

When we were on our way out into the playground after lunch Angela grabbed me by the arm.

"Charlie," she said, and my heart sank when I saw the gleeful expression on her face. "Come with me. I've had a fabulous idea."

She dragged me along the corridor towards the changing rooms at the end. There was nobody around at this hour as they were all outside. Angela shoved me down on a bench beside the girls' lockers and sat beside me.

"What's first lesson this afternoon?" she said, making her eyes go all narrow.

"Games," I said at once. "It's Tuesday, isn't it? It's games all afternoon."

"Right," said Angela. "And what will happen if we all take half an hour to get changed?"

"Miss March will do her nut," I said. "She only gives us sixty seconds, and then she blows that stupid whistle." I looked into Angela's face, hoping for some sort of a clue. "What are you up to?" I said.

Angela gave me a quick hug. "You and me, Charlie, are going to cause chaos this afternoon. We're going to mix up all the games kits, so that everybody ends up with the wrong shorts and teeshirts and stuff. Can you imagine what it'll be like? It'll be a right old shambles."

I could imagine it very clearly and I was horrified at the thought. I stood up quickly and started to argue. But Angela pushed me down again firmly.

"You're not going to say you won't help me, are you?" she said, hands on hips. "Because if you are I'm never going to be your friend again. So you can just make up your mind, Charlie Ellis." And she started pulling shorts and teeshirts and plimsolls out of people's lockers and muddling them up in a heap on the floor.

And do you know, for once in my life it didn't take long for me to make up my mind. I sat there thinking about all the things she had ever done to get me into trouble, and all the nasty tricks she'd played on me in the past and I found it wasn't such a hard decision, after all. I was better off without her, if only I could find the courage to tell her so.

I jumped up in a hurry before I had time to change my mind. I took a deep breath and looked her straight in the eyes.

"Well I think it's a stupid idea and it'll just cause trouble for everybody and Miss March will get mad and she's sure to keep us all in until she finds out who did it and for once it's not going to be me that gets the blame because this time you can do your own dirty work. So there."

Angela's mouth had dropped open and she was giving me a real frosty-nosed stare.

"All right," she said. "If that's the way you want it. But you'll be sorry, Miss Hoity-toity Ellis. Don't say I didn't warn you."

Angela started rummaging round in the lockers again and I scuttled off down the corridor as fast as I could to the playground, feeling relieved at my escape. And when I got outside I found that nice new girl Nicola Daley sitting all by herself on the wall in the sunshine. She's tall and skinny like me and she's got lovely long shiny brown hair and she's going to be a dancer when she grows up. Anyway, she gave me such a nice big smile when she saw me that I went over and sat beside her.

"Where did you live before you moved here?"
I said, to start a conversation.

"Yewesly," she told me, with a giggle. "It's
near Manchester. Funny name for a place, isn't
it?"

"Not half," I agreed. "There was a young lady
from Yewesly. . ." But I had to stop there
because I couldn't think of a rhyme.

"Who always would breakfast on muesli," said
Nicola. And we both burst out laughing.

So we sat there on the wall giggling away like
anything together and making up a funny poem
to send in my next letter to Uncle Barrie, and the
last line was so awful I knew my Uncle Barrie
would love it.

'There was a young lady from Yewesly,
Who always would breakfast on muesli.
When asked for her diet,
She said 'You should try it,
It's muesli, in Yewesly, usually.'

By the time the bell went we were the best of
friends, and we were enjoying ourselves so much
that I'd forgotten all about Angela and her latest
plot. It was only when Miss March blew her
whistle in the corridor that I remembered, and

my stomach suddenly rolled over as if it was full of live eels.

"You have sixty seconds to change, starting from NOW!" bellowed Miss March, and everybody rushed to their lockers and started pulling out their games kit.

"Hey, this isn't my teeshirt," somebody called out.

"I've got the wrong shorts," squealed somebody else.

Everybody started shrieking and yelling and fighting and snatching things from one another and chucking plimsolls around and in no time at all it was absolute pandemonium. I looked for Angela and there she was, right in the middle of the fun, giggling helplessly and shouting "Who's got my bloomin' teeshirt?" at the top of her voice.

Well, some of them didn't half look daft, I can tell you. Angela had even mixed up some of the boys' things with ours, and she was dancing around in an enormous pair of baggy shorts that could only have belonged to Laurence Parker. That awful Delilah Jones, who is by far the tallest girl in the class, was struggling into a skimpy little teeshirt that hardly came down to her tummy button. Jane Baxter, who's really tiny, had shorts almost down to her ankles and a huge pair of plimsolls that flopped about like flippers when she tried to walk. And they were all making so much noise you could hardly hear Miss March's whistle.

"Get out here at once," stormed Miss March from the corridor, and everybody scrambled towards the door.

I had been so busy watching the others that I hadn't even started getting changed myself. I quickly pulled off my skirt and blouse and grabbed at the stuff in my locker, dreading the sight of what Angela had selected for me.

The games kit in my locker was all my own. I stared at the clothes, astonished. I checked the name labels and they all said Charlotte Ellis and I was baffled. Why hadn't Angela mixed up my things as well? I very soon found out.

Miss March was stamping her feet and blowing her whistle like mad by now and everybody had given up trying to sort out the mess and was tumbling out into the corridor. And it was even funnier out there because the boys all started to hoot with laughter when they saw the girls and the girls all screamed and giggled when they caught sight of the boys and the noise was unbelievable.

Laurence Parker was the funniest. He had struggled into the tiniest pair of shorts you ever saw and his big fat belly was sticking out at the top. He had ripped the teeshirt when putting it on and it hung in tatters from his shoulders like the Incredible Hulk's.

"SILENCE!" roared Miss March suddenly, and everybody went quiet.

"Form two lines," she snapped, and everybody shuffled into place, the boys down one side of the corridor and the girls down the other. I joined the end of the girls' line behind Nicola Daley, who had one toe in a very small plimsoll and the other foot in one that looked as if it would fit my dad.

There was a long silence while Miss March glared at us all. All you could hear was her snorting like a dragon. I expected sparks to come flying out of her nose at any minute.

Then she started walking down between the lines, inspecting everybody like a sergeant major in the army, and you could see people's knees tremble as she stopped at each one.

Finally she reached me. She looked me up and down in silence and then she suddenly grabbed me by the shoulder and peered at the name tags in the back of my teeshirt and shorts. Her mouth went into a grim line and that's when it hit me like a ton of bricks. I was the only person in the whole class wearing my own things. My dear friend Angela had done it again.

"That wasn't very clever of you, Charlotte Ellis," grated Miss March through teeth like tombstones. "It's perfectly clear who is responsible for this . . . this . . . *riot* this afternoon. You will all change back into your ordinary clothes at once, and we will have a free activities afternoon instead of games." She looked at me as if I was the nastiest little creature she had ever set eyes on.

"Charlotte Ellis will stay here and sort out this mess. She will put everybody's things exactly where she found them, even if it takes her all day. And there will be no more games for Miss Ellis for the rest of the term."

My face went scarlet. I could see Angela

grinning like a shark at the front of the line. I felt like punching her right in the nose, I can tell you.

"Please, Miss March," I said quickly. "It wasn't me. It was . . . it was . . ."

"Well?" said Miss March, folding her arms and waiting.

But I closed my mouth tight and tears pricked the back of my eyelids. I found I couldn't tell tales, even on somebody as horrible as Angela. I suppose I'm stupid, but that's the way it is.

So everybody else had a lovely afternoon, reading library books, drawing and painting, and working at hobbies like sewing and knitting and weaving and stuff. And I spent the rest of the day sorting out all the games kit. It was an awful job and it took me hours. Only one thing kept me going while I worked. I would walk home after school with my nice new friend Nicola Daley and tell that Angela Mitchell to go and jump in the river.

Things never work out the way you want them to. When the bell finally went I put the last pair of plimsolls thankfully into the right locker and went for my coat. And there was Nicola coming out of the cloakroom, chatting and smiling away, arm in arm with Angela.

"Walk home with us, Charlie?" invited Angela cheerfully, offering her other arm as if nothing had happened.

"I'd rather walk home with a crocodile," I snapped. I meant it, too. At least with a crocodile you always know whose side it's on.

Chapter Seven

If there's one thing Angela can't stand it's me being better than her at anything. And spoiling my lovely party dress was one of the nastiest things she ever did.

I had made the dress for the Autumn Fête, which we have at school every year in October to raise money for sports equipment and stuff. The funny thing is, we never seem to get any new sports equipment, and I bet you anything you like the parents and teachers spend all the money on the wine and cheese party they have afterwards.

Anyway, the best part of the day is the children's fancy dress competition, and you should just see the brilliant prizes they give. Every year they choose a different theme, nursery rhyme characters or TV advertising or something like that, and the rule is that all the costumes have to be home-made. The theme this year was 'Autumn' and I racked my brains for ages without any success. There was only a week left when at last I had an idea.

My mum keeps all her scraps of fabric that she has left from dressmaking and curtains and stuff, and I was rummaging around in the box among the silks and cottons and velvets when I came across a big piece of the most autumny-looking material you ever saw. If was soft and shiny, with a swirly pattern of misty shapes in red and orange and gold and brown. I stared at it for a minute, then I folded it over my arm and went to find my mum.

"Yes, it's nice, isn't it," she said, chopping apples at the kitchen table. "I bought it in a remnant sale years ago. Pity I never got round to doing anything with it."

"Can I have it, please, mum?" I said, sliding my arm round her waist and putting on a pleading look like Daniel does when you're eating sausages. "It'll make a lovely costume for the fancy dress party. The Queen of Autumn, I'm going to be."

"What a nice idea," said my mum. "The colours are perfect. Of course you can have it. But I don't want to find my sewing-box in a mess. Put everything back when you've finished." I gave my mum a smacking great kiss on the cheek.

"Thanks, mum," I said. "You're my best friend."

"I thought Angela was," said my mum with a smile.

"She's not any more," I said, scowling. "I'm sick of her and her rotten jokes. I'm not playing with her ever again."

"You've said that hundreds of times," grinned my mum, and went back to her apples.

I was still mad at Angela over that chocolate cake. It really was a horrible trick. I had called round to see her the evening before, and had found her in the kitchen, sticking chocolate drops into the icing of a big scrumptious-looking chocolate gateau. Chocolate cake is my favourite kind, especially with chocolate butter cream and chocolate icing and chocolate buttons on top.

"Wow," I said. "What a fabulous cake."

Angela put her head on one side as she placed

the last chocolate drop in the icing. Then she slid the cake towards me across the table.

"Have a slice, if you like," she said.

I gazed at the cake doubtfully. "No, I'd better not," I said. "Your mum might not want it cut into yet."

"Don't be silly," said Angela, sitting on the lid of the chest freezer and swinging her legs. "She won't mind. She makes them all the time, you know she does. She likes people to eat them. Go on, Charlie, have a bit. I can see you're dying to."

I suppose my greed must have got the better of my doubts because I got a knife and cut myself a big wedge. Angela watched me tucking in and there was such a sly expression on her face that I began to feel very uncomfortable.

"Aren't you having any?" I asked, my mouth full of butter cream filling.

"No fear," she said. "My mum will go up the wall. She made that cake specially for the fête on Saturday. You won't half catch it when she sees it now."

My eyes bulged out of my head and I choked half to death. The cake suddenly tasted like something off the compost heap and I pushed the half-eaten slice hastily away from me. I was wiping my chocolatey fingers on my hanky when Auntie Sally came in. She gave a little shriek of horror when she saw the cake.

"Angela!" she said. "I told you not to eat any of that cake. I told you it was for the fête. You never listen to a thing I say."

Angela put on a hurt expression. "It wasn't me," she declared virtuously. "I never touched it, honest. Did I, Charlie?"

My throat went dry and my face went red. I felt like opening the freezer and shoving her in and holding her down until her bottom froze.

"It was me, Auntie Sally," I gulped. "I'm sorry. I didn't know it was for the fête."

Auntie Sally looked at Angela and then at me. She must have seen how upset I was.

"Angela should have told you," she sighed at last. "Never mind, Charlie. I can always make another one. And you might as well finish that piece, now you've started it."

But somehow I wasn't hungry any more. I turned and ran for the door and I was almost home when Angela caught up with me.

"Wait, Charlie," she called. "It was only a joke."

"Some joke," I shouted, glaring at her. "You can just keep your jokes to yourself in future, because I'm not playing with you any more."

"Please yourself," shrugged Angela. "See if I care." And she flounced off home with her nose in the air.

Well, you can imagine how surprised I was when I was in my room cutting up that nice material for my costume and I heard Angela's voice downstairs. I quickly bundled the cloth into a drawer and picked up a book, pretending to read. After a few minutes Angela appeared in the doorway, looking sheepish and holding out one of her most cherished possessions. The lovely peacock's tail feather that she got when she went to Dorset for her holidays.

"I don't want to talk to you," I said grumpily.

"Please, Charlie. I've brought you my best feather," she said humbly. "To say I'm sorry and can we be friends." She gazed at me with those big blue eyes. "I'm not going to be horrible to you any more, Charlie. Honest."

"I don't believe you," I said. "Just get lost, will you?"

Angela took a couple of steps into the room "I mean it, Charlie," she said earnestly. "I know I've been rotten to you sometimes. But a person can change, can't they?" And she looked so sorry for herself I hadn't the heart to be cross any more.

"All right then," I said, a bit grudgingly. "But the very next time you do a thing like that . . ." I took the feather and put it in a jar on the window sill where the sunshine could light up the colours.

Angela took a flying leap on to my bed and trampolined in delight. Just when I was expecting my mum to start shouting about all the thumping and banging, she flopped down flat on her back and lay staring at the ceiling.

"What are you wearing for the fancy dress party?" she asked casually. I eyed her suspiciously. Now I knew why she was so keen to make friends.

"I haven't made my mind up yet," I fibbed quickly, crossing my fingers behind my back. I certainly had no intention of telling her my idea. She was quite capable of pinching it herself.

"It's ever such a hard subject," complained

Angela, screwing up her face. "I've thought and thought and I still can't think of a thing. What does autumn make you think of, Charlie?"

I looked out of the window into the back garden where my dad was filling another basket with apples from our tree. Daniel was happily chewing one to bits on the lawn.

"Apples," I said. "You could go as an apple."

Angela sat bolt upright and stared at me.

"What do you mean, I could go as an apple? How could you make an apple costume? Don't be so bloomin' stupid."

"It would be easy," I said, thinking hard. "You could cut two great big enormous apple shapes out of cardboard. You could join them together with little straps at the shoulders and sides. You know, like a sandwich-board man. You could paint the card all lovely red and green apple colours. You could even make a hat out of a tube of paper and paint it to look like a stalk."

Angela's eyes widened. "And I could have green paper leaves, growing out of the stalk," she said, getting excited. "It would be great. Charlie, you're a genius."

She leapt off the bed and started dancing

about. Then she came over and gave me a hug.

"But what about you, Charlie?" she said. "What about your costume?"

"Oh, don't worry. I'll think of something," I said. The less she knew about that, the better.

Well, of course I had to help her with the costume, because she's pretty useless at that sort of thing. So we went down into the garden to find my dad and ask him for some cardboard.

He found us a huge flat box that the new wardrobe kit had been delivered in, and he cut out the two big apple shapes for us with his Stanley knife. We carried them upstairs to my room and spread some newspapers out on the carpet to stop my mum from having hysterics. Then we got busy with the nice thick poster paints that my Uncle Barrie sent me last Christmas.

We made the apple rosy red on one side and a sort of yellowy green on the other and it really did look great. When the paint was dry we stapled some strips of card to the tops and sides of the shapes and Angela tried the costume on. And I couldn't help rolling about laughing when I saw her, with only her head and her feet sticking out.

"Come on, Charlie," she said, grinning at me. "Let's go and show your dad."

She had to go sideways through the door and down the stairs and she kept bumping into things and saying "Ooops." We were helpless with the giggles by the time we reached the garage, and my dad made us even worse.

"I can see you're going to live appley ever after," he told Angela. And she lurched crazily round the garage, making Daniel bark his head off.

So off she went home, as pleased as anything with her costume, and she took my big pot of strong glue with her so she could have a go at making a stalk hat and some leaves.

"I'll bring it back when I've finished with it," she promised.

I hardly saw Angela at all that week. Every evening after school I went straight home and worked on my costume, and I didn't half enjoy myself, all cosy and peaceful in my room with the radio on and Daniel snoozing on a rug beside the radiator.

I'm not much good at sewing, so all I did with my mum's material was make a simple tunic by folding it in half and making a hole in the middle for my head. The tunic came right down to my feet and I fastened it round the waist with a gold dressing gown cord my dad lent me. There was a spare bit of material left to make a short matching cloak, and I sewed on some bits of gold velvet ribbon for the ties at the front.

And now came the nicest part of all. I borrowed my mum's big shopping basket and went out into the country lanes round the edge of the village and I started to collect all the autumn fruits and berries and nuts and dried flowers I could find. There were rose hips and hawthorn berries and conkers and hazelnuts and acorns. There were long trailing strands of some sort of creeper with fluffy white seed heads. There were ears of corn and barley and all sorts of other stuff I didn't know the names of. I brought them all home and set to work with a sharp needle and some strong thread and I made a great pile of the most beautiful jewellery you ever saw.

I made garlands to hang round my neck like the Hawaiian girls do, only mine were made out of dried flowers and grasses. I strung together long necklaces of rose hips and hawthorn berries, and did the same with the acorns and conkers after my dad had drilled holes in them for me with his Black and Decker. I made bangles and bracelets and girdles and even things to go round my ankles. And you should have seen how all those lovely reds and browns and golds and yellows glowed together like precious stones.

Last of all I made a golden crown. I cut it out of card and covered it with gold foil and decorated it with flowers and nuts and berries and ears of wheat. Angela still hadn't brought back my pot of glue, but my dad lent me a tube of superglue which worked even better.

Every day at school Angela would say "Have you finished your costume yet, Charlie?" and every day I shook my head. She was dying to know what it was, but I wouldn't tell her a thing. She could find out on Saturday, when it would be too late for her to pinch my idea.

I finished the costume on Friday evening. I put the final touches to the crown and dressed myself up in the whole outfit. I was grinning at my reflection in the mirror when my dad popped his head round the edge of my door.

"Wow," he said. "You don't half look

smashing. Hey, Liz!" he bellowed down the stairs. "Come and get an eyeful of our Charlie. She's a right bobby-dazzler."

I looked in the mirror and I knew he was right. I don't quite know what it was, but I had never looked so nice in my whole life. Something about my dark hair and suntanned face and brown eyes seemed to set off the autumn colours of my costume and make them glow even brighter. I couldn't wait for Saturday to come and I was sure I would win a prize.

Saturday morning was chaotic with everybody dashing about all over the place. My mum's kitchen was so full of sliced bread you could hardly move. Auntie Sally came round to help bake the scones and the fairy cakes, and she brought with her another chocolate gateau like the one I'd cut a chunk out of.

And do you know, she never said one word about the first one. She only gave me a wink and a quick smile and I could have hugged her. I sometimes can't help wishing that Angela was as nice as her mother.

I did my best to help with the sandwiches and things, but I kept on being told to get out of the way. So in the end I went outside into the garden to help my dad instead.

It was one of those beautiful autumn days when the air is warm and still and the light is sort of golden and everything in the garden looks pleased with itself. My dad was sweeping up the fallen leaves and putting them in a big pile at the end of the garden, and Daniel was bouncing about chasing the broom and barking and diving into the heap of leaves looking for imaginary rabbits. I got a rake out of the shed and gave them a hand for a while, and it was much nicer than being in that hot steamy kitchen.

My dad went off and got us all some fish and chips for lunch and we ate them in the garden straight out of the paper to save the washing-up, which I think is the very nicest way to eat fish and chips. Angela and her dad came back from delivering cakes to the tea tent and joined us in the garden and it was like a party.

At last it was time to get dressed for the fête. We decided it was better for Angela and me to walk to school so we wouldn't spoil our costumes, so my mum and Auntie Sally and Uncle Jim went off in the yellow Mini, leaving my dad to follow later with us kids. Angela ran next door to get into her costume, and I hurried upstairs to get myself ready.

I was just settling my crown more firmly on my head when I heard this funny scraping and thumping noise on the stairs and Angela appeared, easing herself sideways round the door. I started to giggle as soon as I saw her.

She had green tights on and green shoes and she had completed the apple costume with a green stalk hat. A big bunch of green paper leaves dangled from the stalk around her face, which she had also painted green. She was carrying my big pot of glue in her hand.

"You look great," I said admiringly, turning from the mirror to look at her properly.

"Thanks, Charlie," she grinned, "I've brought your glue back. Where shall I put it?" And then she gave a long whistle through her teeth as she suddenly noticed my costume.

She stared at me for a long time without saying a word and her eyes went all glittery and strange. She came a bit closer and stared harder and I felt like laughing even more because somebody in a cardboard apple outfit with their face painted green looks ever so funny when they get mad.

And Angela was mad, I could tell. She was so mad she was almost spitting.

"So this is what you've been up to," she hissed furiously. "You sneaky cat, you never said a word about it." She stamped her feet like a rhinoceros about to charge.

And then something awful happened. She sort of lurched towards me with that big open pot of glue in her hands and to this day I still don't know if it was deliberate or whether she tripped on the corner of the carpet but somehow she managed to tip the whole jarful right down the front of my dress.

I looked down at myself, speechless. A big dollop of glue rolled down my skirt and dripped onto my sandals.

"Ooh, Charlie," said Angela. "I'm ever so sorry." She grabbed a box of tissues from my dressing table and started to dab at the worst bits, but all she did was smear the glue even further.

"Get out," I said, clenching my fists. And she began to edge herself out of the door.

"What a shame," she said. "I'd better go to the fête by myself. I don't suppose you'll be going now, will you?" I picked up my hairbrush and threw it at her, but she was already sliding sideways out of my room and down the stairs.

I stood there for a minute, breathing hard to try and calm myself down. I don't know when I've been more upset. I felt like running after her and tearing her hair out and jumping up and down on her stupid green face. My lovely costume that I'd worked so hard on was totally ruined, and there was nothing I could do about it.

My eyes suddenly filled with tears and a great big horrible lump came into my throat. I dashed down the stairs and into the garden shouting for my dad but I couldn't find him anywhere and the sobs started to come faster and faster and in the end I flung myself down into the big heap of leaves and howled my head off.

My dad found me there a couple of minutes later.

"There, there, bonny lass," he said, kneeling besides me and patting my shoulder helplessly. "What's brought all this on?"

I sat up and flung my arms around his neck and blurted out the whole story, but it was so muffled by the sobs and the hiccups and the leaves that at first he didn't seem to understand.

"Glue? What glue?" he said. "Angela what? She spilt it on your dress?" He gave me his big hanky and I mopped my face. I blew my nose hard and told him all over again what had happened.

"Maybe she didn't do it on purpose," he said, not sounding very convinced. He helped me to my feet and then stepped back to look at me. I didn't half feel stupid standing there covered in leaves from head to foot.

"Charlie," said my dad, smiling broadly all over his face. "Your friend has done you a good turn. She hasn't spoilt your costume at all. She's made it even better."

I looked down at my dress and my tears suddenly vanished like magic when I saw what he meant. Hundreds and hundreds of autumn leaves had stuck to the glue and the front of my skirt was covered in them. They looked just perfect, all shades of gold and red and orange and brown, and the best thing was that they were real leaves. Much nicer than any old dress material.

My dad picked up my crown from where it had rolled away into the flower bed and put it back on my head.

"Hang on, pet," he said. "I'll get the rest of the glue." In no time at all he was back with the jar of glue in his hand and he helped me to stick more leaves to the sides and the back of my skirt until I was covered in them from my waist to my feet.

"That'll show them," he said, looking at me with his head on one side. "You're the bonniest Queen of Autumn I've ever seen. Now let's get a move on. The judging starts in ten minutes."

So we dragged Daniel away from his bone and got his lead on him and hurried along to the school field with me rustling like mad and shedding leaves at every step. And I was just in time to join the end of the procession as they paraded around the edge of the judge's arena.

There were clowns and pirates and cowboys and Indians and hardly anybody had taken any notice of the autumn theme. As soon as I got near the judge's table I knew they liked me because they made me stop and turn round in front of them and Miss Collingwood asked me all sorts of questions about how I had made the costume and whether the leaves had been my own idea.

"A friend helped me," I said, and they nodded and smiled and said how ingenious it was. Then at last the headmistress went to the microphone to announce the winners.

"Perhaps 'Autumn' was rather a difficult theme," she began. "But I'm very pleased to see that one or two people have made a real effort to meet the challenge. Third prize goes to Mark Adamson, as a haystack."

Everybody clapped and cheered as little Mark Adamson from Form One, baled up in straw from head to foot, walked out to collect his prize.

"Second prize," Miss Collingwood went on, "goes to Angela Mitchell, Form Five, for her extremely clever apple costume." The crowd whistled and stamped and you should have seen the way that Angela Mitchell danced about and showed off.

Then we all held our breath as Miss Collingwood looked at the bit of paper in her hand. Everybody went quiet, waiting to hear the name of the winner.

"The judges are all agreed on the winner," said Miss Collingwood, smiling. "And we have no hesitation in awarding First Prize to Charlotte Ellis, for her delightful Queen of Autumn. We particularly liked the way she used the natural fruits and flowers and leaves of the season to decorate her costume."

The crowd all clapped like mad and I felt myself go all pink with pride and delight, right there in front of all those people. I could see my dad going even pinker and my mum looking dead pleased and smug.

And then I looked at Angela, and I found a huge grin spreading over my face because she was tearing off her apple costume and ripping it to shreds and jumping up and down on it.

The prize turned out to be four tickets for a London pantomime, with fifty pounds cash to spend on a slap-up meal afterwards.

"We'll take Angela, shall we?" said my mum,

as we strolled happily home with Daniel later that afternoon. "To use up the spare ticket?"

"Not likely," said my dad. "I wouldn't take her if she was the last person on earth."

"I'd rather take a rattlesnake," I said, and my dad gave a snort of laughter.

In the end we took the new girl, Nicola Daley, and we all had the time of our lives. Angela went wild when she heard about it. But I didn't care. She only got what she deserved, after all.

My Best Fiend

Angela is Charlie's best friend, or best fiend as Charlie accidently wrote in her school essay. But fiend is probably a better word, as it's Angela's so-called marvellous ideas that always get Charlie into trouble, like putting a spider in Miss Menzies' sandwich, plastering glue all over Laurence Parker's chair and, most fiendish of all, setting fire to her father's garage . . .

THE FIEND NEXT DOOR

Living next door to Angela is a mixed
blessing for Charlie. Angela is always
having fiendish ideas that get Charlie
into trouble – big trouble – like
hijacking the milkman's float, locking
Miss Bridge in the gym shed, and calling
the fire brigade to come and rescue
Charlie. But in the end Charlie gets her
own back with a vengeance.